Acting Edition

The Grown-Ups

by Skylar Fox & Simon Henriques

ISBN 978-0-573-71000-1

www.concordtheatricals.com
www.concordtheatricals.co.uk

FOR PRODUCTION INQUIRIES

UNITED STATES AND CANADA
info@concordtheatricals.com
1-866-979-0447

UNITED KINGDOM AND EUROPE
licensing@concordtheatricals.co.uk
020-7054-7298

Each title is subject to availability from Concord Theatricals Corp., depending upon country of performance. Please be aware that *THE GROWN-UPS* may not be licensed by Concord Theatricals Corp. in your territory. Professional and amateur producers should contact the nearest Concord Theatricals Corp. office or licensing partner to verify availability.

This work is published by Samuel French, an imprint of Concord Theatricals Corp.

THE GROWN-UPS was first produced by Nightdrive (Skylar Fox and Simon Henriques, co-artistic directors) and Chloe Joy Ivanson in Greenpoint, Brooklyn in July 2021. The production was directed by Skylar Fox; the associate director and production stage manager was Cristina Villalobos Ureña; the technical director and rain designer was Adam Wyron; the lighting designer was Christopher Annas-Lee; the props designer and set dresser was Emily Elyse Everett; the costume designer was Abby Melick; and the dramaturg was Jared Bellot. The cast was as follows:

LUKAS .... Simon Henriques
CASSIE.................................... Chloe Joy Ivanson
BECCA.................................... Emily Elyse Everett
MAEVE.................................... Abby Melick
AIDAN .... Justin Phillips

Roles were understudied by Raka Dey (Cassie), Skylar Fox (Lukas and Aidan), and Jessie Kenner Tidball (Becca and Maeve).

CHARACTERS

LUKAS – (early twenties, white) is pumped to be back this summer

CASSIE – (early twenties, not white*) is excited to be joining this summer

BECCA – (early twenties, white) is honestly thrilled to be back this summer

MAEVE – (early twenties, white) is literally sooo jazzed to be back this summer you guys

AIDAN – (late twenties, white) has a lot of new responsibilities this summer

AUTHORS' NOTES

Everyone in this play talks pretty fast. (Except when they don't, or can't.) Virtuosity is social currency at camp.

A dash (–) indicates someone being cut off.
A slash (/) in a line indicates where the line after should overlap.
An ellipsis (...) indicates someone trailing off.

The transitions between scenes should feel like all of the light of several days compressed into a microsecond. They should feel like the horror of time passing: quiet, ambivalent, unfair.

This play was originally performed around a campfire in our little backyard in Brooklyn, New York during the COVID-19 pandemic. Ten audience members at a time sat in a tight circle with the actors, drinking beer and making s'mores together. A drone flew over the buildings of our neighborhood into our yard each night. Rain started and stopped on command. You don't have to do all this in your production, but maybe think of little ways you can take an audience out of their usual theatrical environment, and gently move them somewhere both familiar and strange enough that they're uniquely susceptible to stories.

---

*The actor who originally created this role is half Korean, half white. Cassie should not be played by a white actor, but we do not want to limit who can play the role beyond that. Consider how the different perspectives and experiences of your cast shape the dynamics of the group of counselors.

The Grown-Ups was originally created with
Emily Elyse Everett, Chloe Joy Ivanson,
Abby Melick, and Justin Phillips.

Scene One

(A campfire in a clearing, surrounded by camping chairs and logs. When the audience enters the clearing, one counselor, **LUKAS**, *is sitting, tending the fire. It's dusk. He looks a bit lost in his thoughts, and definitely doesn't notice the audience. Behind us is a cabin. Occasionally,* **LUKAS** *takes a folded piece of paper out of his pocket, unfolds it, reads it, and puts it away again. Once we're all seated, he takes the piece of paper out of his pocket and reads it to himself one final time. A somber moment. He holds the paper out toward the fire, and the end catches. He doesn't let go as it begins to burn. He stares at it. He changes his mind. He starts blowing on it hard, then drops it on the ground and starts stomping on it until it's put out. He hears voices coming from the cabin. The paper is now a sad, dirty, part-burnt mess of what it was. He quickly hides it in his pocket and tries to act natural.)*

*(***BECCA** *and* **CASSIE** *enter from the cabin behind us, mid-conversation.* **BECCA** *has a sticker on her shirt.* **CASSIE** *is spiraling a bit.)*

CASSIE. I feel like such an idiot.

BECCA. It's totally normal.

CASSIE. Yeah?

BECCA. Totally.

CASSIE. She just, like, wouldn't stop crying, and I kept asking, "What's wrong? What's wrong?" But she just kept saying, / "It's an emergency!"

BECCA. "It's an emergency"? It's almost never an emergency. They just know that's what they have to say to get the phone.

CASSIE. Right, I guess she really made it seem like an emergency? She kept threatening to eat a rock. But I'm probably just easily manipulated.

BECCA. It might have felt like an emergency. Not a lot of things are emergencies, but a lot of things feel like emergencies –

CASSIE. I feel that.

BECCA. – to seven-year-olds. It's our job to tell the difference.

LUKAS. Becca!

BECCA. Lukas!

(Then, introducing **CASSIE.***)* Lukas, Cassie.

LUKAS. Cassie.

CASSIE. Lukas. *(To herself, to help her remember.)* Lukas Lukas Lukas. Okay.

LUKAS. No presh. It's a lot of names.

(A moment. Then, to **BECCA:***)*

Oh Yay No Way?

BECCA. Ooh okay. My No Way is bug bites. My Oh Yay is it just feels amazing to be back.

LUKAS. *(Noticing the sticker on* **BECCA***'s shirt.)* You got an appreciation!

BECCA. *(Proud.)* Yeah. Julie was sitting off to the side in World Games, so I gave her a little pep talk and she ended up joining in and feeling really confident, and then she stuck this on me at Wash Up. Which felt cool.

Did you...?

(**LUKAS** *humbly pulls up his sleeve to show two stickers on his bicep.)*

Whoa.

LUKAS. *(Self-deprecating.)* It was the twins. They do everything together.

BECCA. Right. Totally.

LUKAS. Is Maeve still coming?

BECCA. Yeah she got held up. Alyssa was having a Growing Moment.

(Defining the term for **CASSIE.***)* First period.

LUKAS. Or it can be anything pubescent. New body smells, nocturnal emishies, Hair Down There...

BECCA. So Maeve stayed behind to help out.

LUKAS. *(To* **CASSIE.***)* She's really good at that stuff. Have you met Maeve yet?

CASSIE. I think I noticed her at orientation.

LUKAS. Yeah, that was probably her.

BECCA. *(Kind of changing the subject.)* But you? Oh Yay No Way?

LUKAS. Oh! My No Way is I didn't realize Chef Dan was retiring. I never got to say goodbye. But Oh Yay, I'm trying to start doing a Dawn Diary, and when I mentioned it to my cabin they were all really into it, and they're gonna do it with me.

BECCA. Cool.

LUKAS. Cassie?

CASSIE. Oooh, um, okay! Cool. My Oh Yay is / definitely that –

BECCA. Start with No Way!

CASSIE. What?

BECCA. You should do your No Way first, so you get to end on something positive.

CASSIE. But then shouldn't it be called No Way Oh Yay?

(A long pause. **LUKAS** *and* **BECCA** *look, blank-faced, at* **CASSIE**, *then each other, then* **CASSIE**.*)*

LUKAS. *(Sincere.)* You can do whatever order you want.

(Pause.)

CASSIE. Well, my No Way is I gave in and let one of my campers use the phone to call her parents, and now my entire cabin wants to, and I don't know how to explain why she could but they can't without just saying, "I'm weak and I'm sorry."

LUKAS. That's real. Did you do the Questions?

CASSIE. I completely forgot them. She was crying so loud, like a little human car alarm. I couldn't think.

BECCA. It happened to me too when we first started doing them. When we were campers you just couldn't call until Half-Way Day, no exceptions. But then everyone started getting their kids cell phones, so we confiscated the cell phones, but then the parents started sending their kids with two cell phones, so we just gave in for the sake of keeping camp phone-free. But we still try to help them choose to be fully present at camp.

LUKAS. That's what the Questions are for.

BECCA. They really work. Camp Director Linda's husband used to be a psychologist.

LUKAS. *(To* **CASSIE.***)* He used to do these evaluations of us before our parents could drop us off.

BECCA. I think they just did that because of the Neversleeper.

CASSIE. The Neversleeper?

BECCA. Oh my god! You don't know about the Neversleeper! We get to tell you!

LUKAS. I mean, you should tell it. You were there.

BECCA. You were there.

LUKAS. Yeah, but you were *there* there.

BECCA. Okay. So, we were seven years old / and –

*(***MAEVE** *enters. She is covered in, like, thirty appreciations, on her face, all over.)*

LUKAS. Maeve!

MAEVE. What's up, buttercups?

BECCA. Is Alyssa okay?

MAEVE. Yeah, I gave her a pad, but she was having trouble figuring out how to put it in her underwear, so I went in and showed her, and she was really embarrassed for some reason so I invited all the other girls in and we gathered around her stall and held hands and started chanting her name. And then she came out, and everyone held each other and screamed and then we did a one-song dance party and then they went to bed. And now I'm here! Hi.

BECCA. This is Cassie.

MAEVE. Oh yeah I noticed you at orientaysh!

CASSIE. I noticed you too at...orientaysh. When you were doing the songs. So many songs!

MAEVE. Blah. I can't really sing, but I've got a lot of spirit!

(A moment.)

MAEVE. *(Very sincere.)* It's literally so good to see you guys. There hasn't been a moment to like, stop and feel that.

LUKAS. Entonces, ¿todavía chupa huevos tu español o te arreglaron? *[So does your Spanish still suck, or did they fix you?]*

MAEVE. *(In fast, pretty fluent Spanish.)* Que chistoso que preguntas eso porque, qué coincidencia, el Gobierno de Chile me llamó y me hizo prometer a entregarte un mensaje: Tú eres lento, yo soy rápido. ¿Cachai? *[It's so funny that you should ask that because actually the Chilean government got in touch and made me promise to deliver a message to you, which is: You're slow. I'm fast. Get it?]*

*(**LUKAS** smiles. **CASSIE** seems confused.)*

BECCA. *(To **CASSIE**.)* Maeve was in Chile last semester.

CASSIE. Oh. How was it?

MAEVE. I did a lot of hiking. It's beautiful there. And then halfway through the semester I got really, really sad. Like I couldn't move, and had no appetite, so I had no energy, so I never left my dorm. I'd just sit in the dark the whole day and listen to white noise. And then I came back home and got a new therapist and meds aaaaaaand that feels good.

*(**MAEVE** smiles. Pause.)*

CASSIE. I love white noise.

MAEVE. *I* love white noise! White noise buddies!

*(A strange pause. **MAEVE** smiles at **CASSIE**.)*

But how 'bout you? How was your year? Or I guess life? Wanna just do your whole life?

CASSIE. Okay. I was born in Delaware... I was born in Delaware... I went to school. In Delaware... I used to make bracelets...

MAEVE. Awww we make bracelets.

BECCA. We should all make bracelets.

CASSIE. But now my company has a production facility that makes the bracelets.

LUKAS. Your company?

CASSIE. Yeah, it's so stupid. I basically founded it by accident 'cause I started making these bracelets out of recycled plastic when I was on bed rest and it got really out of control.

MAEVE. What were you on bed rest for? If it's okay to ask.

CASSIE. Oh, yeah, I just donated my kidney.

BECCA. Wow.

CASSIE. To this girl on my slalom team. I used to ski slalom.

LUKAS. Like, the Olympics?

CASSIE. I was pre-Olympic. I mean, I don't really know what that means. Everyone who isn't Olympic is pre-Olympic in everything, so...

BECCA. And now you run your business.

CASSIE. Well now I'm in college.

BECCA. What are you studying?

CASSIE. Physics.

MAEVE. Wow.

(Pause. She takes **CASSIE** *in.)*

You're such a real person.

CASSIE. I guess?

MAEVE. Please. Keep going.

CASSIE. Oh uh...
I'm a mentor for Junior Diplomats...
My favorite food is pizza...

LUKAS. *(Genuinely confused.)* How did you end up here?

CASSIE. Hm?

LUKAS. Our parents just sent us here when we were little.
And we kept coming back.
But you...could've done anything. It seems like.
So why are you here??

BECCA. That's so rude! *(To* **CASSIE.***)* We're so happy you're here.

CASSIE. *(Frank.)* You don't have to be happy I'm here. You don't know me yet.

(Pause.)

BECCA. *(Slightly scared but trying to hide it.)* Okay.

MAEVE. We don't have to wait to get to know you better to decide we like you.

CASSIE. You're so optimistic. That's so cool.

AIDAN. *(Entering.)* Phones!

(He wears a walkie-talkie on his waist connected to an earpiece he never takes out of his ear and carries a bucket labeled "Phones." Everyone's attention immediately shifts to him, as he brings the bucket to each **COUNSELOR** *and they grab their phone.)*

LUKAS. Thanks, Aidan.

AIDAN. Just doing my job.

(As they turn on their phones, they all get fully engrossed and ignore **AIDAN**. *As he gives* **CASSIE** *back her phone...)*

Cassie! How was your first real day?

CASSIE. It's intense. Really intense.

AIDAN. Good intense?

CASSIE. Yeah, mostly. Yeah.

AIDAN. Good. Very good.

(More silence, as now everyone is reading their phones for the first time that day.)

Well, my day one was nuts. Have you all noticed how loud it is? How much louder it is around the lake this summer?

BECCA. *(Never looking up from her phone.)* Oh yeah, I guess.

AIDAN. It is! It's louder. Like, listen to it.

(He listens to it. He doesn't like it.)

So first thing I'm in Camp Director Linda's office, and I'm like, "Have you noticed how much louder it is?" And she slides this magazine across her desk, and what am I looking at? I'm looking at a list of the Top Ten Hidden Gems of the Northeast of Real Estate of the Year, for this year. And guess who's number three?

(He waits. No one guesses.)

It's us. It's the lake. So all these houses that have sat around abandoned for so long, you know what people have been doing? They've been buying them. They've been fixing them up. And they've been living in them.

So I'm shocked. I don't even, I don't even know what to say. So I say the only thing I can think to say. "Camp

Director Linda. What the heck?" And CDL is like, here's the deal. I need you. To take the golf cart. And go around the lake to every single house, and make sure they know:

One: Welcome to the neighborhood.

Two: There are kids who swim in this lake. So if you've got a motorboat or jet skis, we'd ask you to cut a wide berth around the buoys.

Three: We've been on this lake for more than a hundred years, and we just try to have fun and be respectful members of the community. We trust you'll do the same. And if there's any problem, I'm the Assistant Camp Director and here's my number.

So, I go to the first house. Nice people. Second house. Respectful. Third house, they invite me in for iced tea. No thank you. Caffeine does not agree with me. House numbers four through seven, no one's home, so –

(**LUKAS** *laughs, looking at his phone.)*

What?

LUKAS. Oh, it's just this pineapple that looks like Dwayne "The Rock" Johnson.

BECCA. Oh, you haven't seen the Pineapple?

AIDAN. Let me see.

(He walks over and looks over **LUKAS'** *shoulder at his phone.)*

I don't see it.

MAEVE. Oooooh you're a Pineapple Person.

AIDAN. I'm a what?

MAEVE. Like, there are two kinds of people. Dwayne People, who see him, and Pineapple People, who don't. There are all these memes about it, and what the different kinds of people "be like." Dwayne People?

(She raises her hand, and all others but **AIDAN** *follow.)*

Looks like it's just you.

CASSIE. And politicians have started doing it? It's political now. Like, Bret Hoskins tweeted something about it?

AIDAN. Does he see it or not?

CASSIE. Very much not. He said something about pulling the wool off America's eyes, and then posted a video of himself shooting a hundred pineapples with an AR-15. And now a bunch of Pineapple People think the pineapple isn't real and was Photoshopped? But like, with a code that's supposed to make you believe... something?

BECCA. Fun fact: Bret Hoskins was a camper here.

CASSIE. *(Noting the slogan on her staff t-shirt.)* Nurturing the leaders of tomorrow.

(Pause. They fall back into their phones.)

AIDAN. House number eight: I ring the doorbell and a little kid answers. Maybe five or six. And I say, "Hello, young man. Are your parents home?" And he says no. And that's when I hear a scream from inside the house. And I say, "Who was that?" And he says, "Brayden." So I go in, and I see Brayden, who's also probably five. He's staring through these two-story glass windows, and I ask if he's okay, and he said he wanted to see if he could break the windows by screaming, and it seems like he can't so he'll have to try another way. I ask him if any grown-ups are home, and he says "Tori." I call out for Tori, and out comes a nine-year-old covered in paint and carrying a big pair of scissors. So I walkie back to Linda and tell her I've been delayed, because I can't leave these kids alone. And I wait there with them for maybe half an hour. Until finally the front door opens and in walk Mom and Dad, who see me and the mom screams and the dad gets in my face shouting, "Who the eff are you? Are you some kind of pervert?" And I say, "Welcome to the neighborhood!" And he says some not very nice things, and I say, "Hey man, I'm not the one who left my kids all alone, I was just trying to do the right thing." And the mom says they weren't all alone, Tori was in charge and I say she's a child and they say they'd rather a child be in charge than a pervert like me. So I go. And by now, this is taking a long time and I need to get back to set up for Friday Festival. I go meet the moonbounce people, and then wash the bottoms of the kayaks, and skim the pool, and at that point I haven't eaten since breakfast, so I go and get some leftovers from dinner and I'm sitting alone in the mess, and I realize: I haven't seen a single camper today. I entirely missed them. I guess that's how this job works. That's how things are now.

(A moment. **LUKAS** *looks up.)*

LUKAS. That sounds tough.

AIDAN. Well it's just how things are now. With great responsibility...

*(***AIDAN** *just stands there staring.)*

LUKAS. Do you wanna join –

AIDAN. Ah, wish I could, but I can't. Kind of you to offer, kind of you to offer, but I've gotta finish passing out these phones, so...

LUKAS. Word.

AIDAN. But hey, maybe tomorrow I'll do you guys last. We'll see.

(He stretches his legs for a moment.)

Don't stay up too late.

(He goes. More silence.)

LUKAS. It *is* louder this summer. *(Shaking his head.)* Rich people.

CASSIE. My parents bought a place on the lake this summer. That's why I'm here.

LUKAS. Oh. That's cool.

(Pause.)

BECCA. We were gonna tell Cassie the Neversleeper.

MAEVE. Ooh, here we go! First scary story of the summer. Phones away.

(Everyone puts their phones away.)

Open hearts.

*(**MAEVE** and **LUKAS** uncross their arms. **CASSIE** is a little confused.)*

LUKAS. *(To **CASSIE**.)* We just don't cross our arms.

BECCA. Any last words?

MAEVE. *(To **CASSIE**.)* Once someone starts a scary story, you can't talk until it's over. You have to stop what you're doing and listen.

BECCA. So. Cassie. This was our first summer at camp. And we were seven. And I just want to say before I go any further that all of this really happened. To us.

We were Chickadees, me and Maeve, and there's another girl in our cabin named Sandy. And she's a little bit quiet, but sweet, and we're all just excited to make new friends.

And the first night, we're all nervous, but our counselor Jocelyn is so nice, and she gets us all to calm down, and we finally fall asleep.

And when we wake up, it's the middle of the night. And we hear something. And we look, and Sandy is sitting straight up in bed, her eyes fully open, and she's singing.

(Singing slowly, quietly.)

EVERYBODY, EVERYBODY, EVERYBODY'S GOT TO GO
EVERYBODY, EVERYBODY, EVERYBODY'S GOT TO GO

And Jocelyn goes over and sits on the edge of her bed and pets her hair and helps her lay back down until she's quiet.

The next day, we ask Sandy about it, and she says she doesn't remember saying or singing anything. But that night, it happens again. And the next morning we sing the song back to her to see if she remembers, and she asks us if we're playing a prank on her, and we promise we're not.

When it happens the third night, Jocelyn can't get Sandy to stop. Everyone's a bit concerned and a bit cranky, because we haven't had a full night's sleep in three days. But we want to make sure we're being really accepting of Sandy, and making space for her to be different, in her way.

So the night after that, we get a big bag of cotton balls from the infirmary, and we stuff them into our ears hard, so that no matter what, she can't wake us up.

And it works! We sleep through the night. But when we wake up, Sandy's gone. And so's all our stuff. All of our bags and clothes and trunks. And the counselors go out to look for her, and she's at the end of the dock, dropping our bags into the lake. And Jocelyn runs down to her and asks...okay this part we weren't there for but this is what we heard from reliable sources...Jocelyn asks her, "Why are you doing that?" Or something. And Sandy turns over her shoulder slowly and whispers...

"They won't need these where they're going."

And Jocelyn realizes that Sandy's still asleep.

The next night, Jocelyn zips Sandy into a sleeping bag so she won't be able to get up, and we all put in our cotton balls, and Jocelyn locks the door. It's getting harder to be nice to Sandy during the day, mostly because we're kind of afraid of her, but we're really trying.

And we're all watching out of the side of our eyes to see if Sandy will go to sleep normally.

And it seems like she does.

But then there's a wiggle,
and her hand slips over the top of the bag,
and onto the zipper,
which slides down the side of the bag slowly,
until it stops.

And then, I don't know how she does this so fast, she runs across the cabin and leaps on top of Jocelyn, who's actually asleep, and we all jump up and run and pull her off of her, and she's so strong, and Jocelyn wakes up and ties Sandy to her bunk for everyone's safety, especially Sandy's.

And we all go to sleep.

And my eyes are closed. And I feel something moving in my mouth. And then my mouth opens wider and wider. And I start choking. And I open my eyes and try to sit up...

But Sandy is kneeling on my chest. And she has her fingers pressing my teeth open. And she's filling my mouth with dirt. And I try to scream but no one can hear me because everyone's ears are plugged. And I throw her off of me. I don't know how I did it, she was so strong, but I guess I didn't want to die I guess.

The next night Sandy isn't in our cabin anymore. Jocelyn tells us Sandy is still a part of our cabin, but she's going to be sleeping somewhere else from now on.

And we didn't know this then, but they actually just didn't let her sleep at all. They tried to call her parents to have them take her home, but none of her emergency contacts were picking up. So they cleared out one of the supply sheds and counselors had to take shifts keeping her awake all the time.

But after a few days, someone slips up. The rumor is they fell asleep in the chair in her room. And Sandy gets up. And gets out. And she comes back to our cabin. And we wake up to smoke and sirens because Sandy lit our cabin on fire.

And we somehow all make it out safe.

And we never saw her again.

(A long silence.)

LUKAS. And I was there too.

But with the boys.

(Silence.)

CASSIE. That sounds really scary.

BECCA. I mean, yeah, it was. I almost died.

But I have enough distance from it now that I can laugh about it.

(Pause. She doesn't laugh.)

We should jump in the lake! Does anyone want to jump in the lake?

MAEVE. I'll go. Lukas?

LUKAS. Let's do it.

BECCA. Cassie?

CASSIE. I shouldn't. I need to get to bed.

BECCA. Okay.

LUKAS. Goodnight.

*(***BECCA*** and* **LUKAS** *leave.* **MAEVE** *hangs back a sec, letting them go ahead.)*

MAEVE. Is everything okay?

CASSIE. Is Becca okay?

MAEVE. Oh, yeah. I mean... Yeah. She used to really not like when other people told the story, but at some point she started telling it, and now like, she can tell it, and hear it, and be scared of it, and survive. And if she can survive that...

CASSIE. It makes her feel powerful.

MAEVE. Or less scared at least.

(Pause.)

CASSIE. *(Confused.)* Was I supposed to jump in the lake?

MAEVE. Do you *wanna* jump in the lake?

CASSIE. Not really. I just always feel like there's something I'm supposed to do in groups and I never know if I'm doing it.

MAEVE. You're doing perfect.

CASSIE. That's good, but then I have no idea why.

(Pause.)

MAEVE. Can I tell you something? I really want you to like it here. This place is really special to me. And you seem special. So...

(Pause.)

I know that's a lot of pressure.

CASSIE. A little bit, yeah.

MAEVE. But you don't have to do anything you don't want to do.

I'm gonna go jump in the lake. And we'd love to have you.

But if not, I'll see you tomorrow.

(She starts to go, then remembers something and turns back.)

Just put out the fire when you're ready to go to sleep. You don't wanna burn the whole forest down.

(She smiles. She leaves. **CASSIE** *watches her go. Then she turns and watches the fire. A flash.)*

Scene Two

(Several days later. **MAEVE** *and* **BECCA** *enter.)*

BECCA. Cassie!

CASSIE. Becca! Maeve!

MAEVE. Cassie!

LUKAS. *(Entering with a cooler.)* Lukas!

I hope everyone's thirsty.

(He sits and starts to pass beers around the circle.)

MAEVE. *(To* **CASSIE.***)* Thanks for starting the fire, babe. How was today?

CASSIE. No one cried, so that's a step forward, right?

BECCA. Totally!

CASSIE. I mean, a bunch of them are still asking to call home. It would be great if, like, at some point, one of you could go over the Questions with me. They're very pathetic when they beg.

LUKAS. Definitely.

CASSIE. *(Turning down a beer.)* Oh, I'm good.

LUKAS. You sure?

CASSIE. I'm not supposed to with my meds.

MAEVE. I mean, my meds *say* that too, but they just say that so you can't sue them if you hurt yourself, or like die.

CASSIE. Uh-huh. Our meds are probably different.

(Pause.)

Soooo, Rachel and I started planning with our cabin for Rainbow Summit. You all better watch out. We're getting ready to kick some serious butt.

BECCA. Oooh, actually, I'm really glad you're excited, but that's kind of not the spirit of Rainbow Summit.

CASSIE. Oh, I mean, I wasn't –

BECCA. There's just a complicated history. We've made a lot of changes. Especially this year.

MAEVE. Yeahhhhh when we were campers, it was Color Wars. But the Iraq War was going on, and a bunch of kids got really into building out the different armies, and there were little generals and little intelligence operatives, and eventually little anti-war protestors doing little die-ins in the Founders Lodge, so they decided the word "war" was maybe too political. So then we had Color Clash. Which they realized sounded kind of...racial. So they changed it to Rainbow Clash, and that's what we've had for a while. But then last year –

LUKAS. The whole thing had been getting more and more competitive for years.

MAEVE. Yeah, and some of the kids really loved that. Really thrived in that environment. But it was making some of them so nervous they couldn't eat, or would fake being sick to get out of it. One girl tried to break her arm with a canoe paddle / so she wouldn't have to play.

BECCA. So we decided to take a step back. And now we're trying the Rainbow Summit, a celebration of community, cooperation, collaboration, civilization –

CASSIE. Right, the twelve Cs. Rachel told me.

*(**AIDAN** enters with the phone bucket.)*

AIDAN. Phones!

(He starts passing them out. People get into their phones.)

BECCA. *(To **CASSIE**.)* What're you all doing your presentation about?

CASSIE. The girls were trying to decide between climate change and horses. So they compromised, and we're doing the effects of climate change on horses.

AIDAN. Ahhh, Compromise. The eleventh C.

LUKAS. They kind of get weaker as they go along.

AIDAN. Nah, the way I see it, compromise is the whole point! Some people wanted to keep it exactly the same, some people wanted to cancel the whole thing, so everyone compromised and we made a new thing that isn't exactly the thing that anyone didn't want. And I...well, I think that's beautiful in a lot of ways. Not everyone sees it that way.

BECCA. *(To* **CASSIE.***)* A lot of counselors didn't come back.

CASSIE. Yeah, when I interviewed, Linda seemed really, um...

LUKAS. Desperate?

CASSIE. Eager. Eager I guess.

MAEVE. It wasn't just Rainbow Clash. There'd been a lot of changes over time, and there weren't hard feelings or anything –

AIDAN. Well, there were some hard feelings. We can be honest. There were some hard feelings and that's okay.

Sometimes things that make something special for you actually make it worse for someone else. And then when you try to make it special for those people, you feel a little less special. And then it's up to you what you wanna do about that.

I mean, when I was a Salamander, I loved Color Wars. I remember lying on the ground, being a human carpet – in those days, the losers had to be servants for the week for the winning color, and the Blues wanted human furniture – and I remember looking up at all the winners around me, and on top of me, and thinking,

"Wow. Now there's something to strive for." And then I grew up. And I got older. And – well, I never did win, but it was so meaningful to have this motivation to...

(He notices the beer.)

Guys. Come on.

MAEVE. What?

AIDAN. Guys. Guys. You know better. You...gah. This is... you know you guys are putting me in a tough position here.

(He points to the cans.)

Right out in the open? A naked transgression?

Now I'm. I'm gonna have to decide. God. I'm gonna have to make a decision about what I'm gonna do about this.

MAEVE. Just be cool Aidan.

AIDAN. *(Very not cool.)* Well, I'd like that very much, to be cool. To just be cool. But if...if...I don't report this...oh boy. Okay. This is not...this is not...

(He closes his eyes and takes a deep breath.)

I've considered my options, and I think the best course of action would be for me to simply remove myself from this situation. So that's what I'm going to do. If we trust you with these kids' lives, I'm just gonna have to trust you with this. Be safe. Don't stay up too late.

(He turns to go.)

LUKAS. You could also join, if you want. It's my bad, I brought the beer, but you can have some. If it'd feel nice to have a breather.

AIDAN. *(Really wanting to stay.)* I... I... I... I... I... This isn't really about what would feel nice. And anyway, there aren't enough chairs, so...

CASSIE. We could probably find a chair.

AIDAN. Well, of course. We have the chair shed.

(He doesn't move.)

CASSIE. But no pressure.

AIDAN. *(Playing it as cool as he can.)* I can get a chair. I'll... I'll go rustle up a chair.

(He goes. Everyone looks at their phones.)

BECCA. Oh no.

LUKAS. He can be chill.

BECCA. No...a bunch of Pineapple People found the address of the guy who posted the picture, and they showed up to his house demanding for him to come out and show them the pineapple for real. They were livestreaming everything, and calling themselves the Truth Squad. And he like, wouldn't come out, or wouldn't show them the pineapple, because I guess he already ate it, so things kind of escalated from there and they lit his house on fire. And his family was inside. And none of them came out.

LUKAS. Whoa.

MAEVE. Oh my god.

CASSIE. Fuck.

BECCA. *(This stands for "Not Camp Appropriate.")* NCA.

CASSIE. Oh, fuck, sorry.

I mean shit.

I mean fuck.

I mean sorry.

LUKAS. It's okay. It's a lot.

CASSIE. Yeah.

(Pause.)

CASSIE. So. Were you close with the counselors who left?

BECCA. Some of them. That's why they had to promote so many younger kids to senior counselor.

LUKAS. We're the only ones from our year left.

CASSIE. That must be weird.

MAEVE. There are always people who don't come back. Becca wasn't going to for a while.

BECCA. But I didn't want to miss our last summer.

MAEVE. And we have a group text. Like they all know about you.

CASSIE. Oh. Cool. Tell them I say hi.

BECCA. And like, Lukas and Shannon are dating. Like, since forever. It's the cutest story. Lukas, you should do the story!

LUKAS. I don't have to...

BECCA. But we want you to! Right? Do the voices!

LUKAS. We're not actually...

It's complicated. Or that's what she said it was.

(He collapses into violent sobs.)

Fuck. And I know that's NCA, but how I feel is NCA!

MAEVE. Lukas –

LUKAS. *(Still weeping.)* Don't pity me! We're just taking some time to pursue our individual journeys, and if the paths of those journeys converge in the future, that's great, and if not, then it was probably never meant to be. And maybe I actually have a higher purpose, apparently? And am the bearer of a prophecy? But I always wake up before I find out what it is. So what am I supposed to do? What am I supposed to do?

(**CASSIE** *gets a phone call and ignores it.* **MAEVE** *moves closer to* **LUKAS**.)

MAEVE. I'm sorry you're in so much pain.

LUKAS. Me too. And I try to channel that pain into empathy and positivity for my boys, because it's not their fault. I think it's working. They're all really coming into their own. Caleb, I mean, night one Caleb drew pubic hair on himself with a Magic Marker because he was the only one who didn't have any, and like, look at him now, you know? When he did that big rope swing off the crag, I like, I teared up. And Anthony R. was like, "That's gay." And I was like, "That's not something we say ever Anthony." And he was like, "No, something being gay means you accept it." And I was like, wow. These boys. These young men. They're gonna change the world.

Because things have to change. And that's what was tough, Cassie. All these changes and people deciding whether or not to stay came down to what do you care about more? Taking the best care of these kids that we can? Or doing things the way we've always done them? And to have all these people who you thought shared your values just leave when they had the opportunity to step up? It's hard. Because I wanna be here. I wanna make things better. And these changes to Rainbow Summit, and athletics –

CASSIE. And the name.

LUKAS. *(Not quite hearing.)* Huh?

CASSIE. You all changed the name of the camp this year, right?

LUKAS. *(Unsure how she knows this.)* Oh. Yeah.

CASSIE. When you Google Indigo Woods, there are a lot of not great local news stories that come up.

MAEVE. The fight got way out of hand. Like, obviously being named after the Wabanaki was really problematic, because like, I mean: this is stolen land. And having a name like that, at a place that's like...like, Indigo Woods is so white.

CASSIE. *(Looking at all the other counselors.)* Yeah, I noticed that.

MAEVE. Yeah. So the name was just bad. For camp culture. And like, all these alums were like –

BECCA. It was insane.

LUKAS. They just refused to acknowledge that having that name was...

CASSIE. ...Racist.

LUKAS. It was. Racist. Yeah. And I think, I guess, a lot of stuff we used to do here was racist as a result, or like... But at the heart of this place I really believe there's something worthwhile. Maybe that's just because I've been coming here so long. But I think it can be meaningful to more people than just us, and I want to figure out how to do that.

CASSIE. Well, I hope you're right. That there's something here that's worth it.

BECCA. We do too.

*(**CASSIE** gets another phone call. She looks at it.)*

MAEVE. You can take that. We'll be quiet.

CASSIE. No, I know, I just...okay. One sec.

(She answers the phone.)

Don't call me.

(She hangs up. Pause.)

Sorry. That was my parents.

LUKAS. Oh. Are you close?

CASSIE. We're working on it. They want me to come home.

MAEVE. Well it means a lot that you want to stay.

CASSIE. Yeah, I don't know. Yeah. I don't really know if I want to talk about it.

BECCA. Okay.

LUKAS. Would this maybe be a good time to go through the Questions? If you're up for it.

CASSIE. Yeah, okay, that sounds good, let's go for it.

LUKAS. I'll be the counselor, you be the camper, okay?

(**CASSIE** *nods.*)

Hey buddy. I'm sorry you're not feeling good. And you know what? I've felt that way before too. If you want to call home, ultimately, that's your choice. But before you do, can we try something that's really helped me when I feel like that?

CASSIE. Okay.

LUKAS. Are you okay to close your eyes? It really helps to close your eyes.

(**CASSIE** *nods and closes her eyes.* **LUKAS** *closes his eyes too.*)

So, what we're gonna do now is I'm gonna ask you some questions, and all you have to do is answer them in a way that is true and honest to your heart. There are no wrong answers. Just your answers. Ready?

CASSIE. Yeah.

(**LUKAS** *takes a deep breath.*)

LUKAS. First, tell me everything you miss about home.

CASSIE. My dog.
My mom.
My dad.
My phone.

My TV.
My bed...

And alone time...

And gum.

(Pause.)

LUKAS. Those things all sound awesome. Can you see them all in your head?

CASSIE. Mhm.

LUKAS. Now imagine yourself getting home from camp at the end of a big, fun summer. Do you think all those things will still be there?

(Pause.)

CASSIE. Yes.

LUKAS. Well that's really cool to know. Now, can you tell me some of the things you like about camp so far?

CASSIE. Crafts.
And archery.
And my new friends.
Snacks...

LUKAS. *(Realizing she is done.)* Wow. Cassie, what do you hope to get out of your summer at Indigo Woods?

*(**CASSIE** thinks.)*

CASSIE. Making peace with the way I am

(Pause.)

And being part of the community.

LUKAS. You don't have to tell me what it is, but can you think of one little thing you can do tomorrow to get you one step closer to your hopes?

CASSIE. I think so.

LUKAS. Okay.

Now that you have that to look forward to, do you think you can hang on for one more day without calling home?

(Pause. **CASSIE** *nods.* **LUKAS** *has his eyes closed and can't see.)*

I know it might feel hard, but do you think you can be brave enough to try?

CASSIE. I nodded.

BECCA. She nodded yes.

LUKAS. Oh, my eyes are closed too. Sorry. It's part of making it really equal.

(They both open their eyes. The magic feels a little broken to **LUKAS.***)*

So, yeah, that's it.

CASSIE. Yeah cool thanks I'll try that.

*(***AIDAN** *re-enters with a chair.)*

AIDAN. What a journey! What a journey. The chair shed...

(He catches his breath.)

...was empty. People are taking chairs out. And just leaving them. In the woods. By the creek. As if there's some kind of chair fairy who collects chairs and brings them back to the chair shed. Which there obviously isn't! So I had to go collect all the chairs and bring them back to the chair shed. But I'm here! I'm here.

(He puts down his chair in the circle. He starts to sit.)

Well, I have to say –

(Before he can sit, his walkie beeps and buzzes in his ear.)

AIDAN. Go for Aidan.

(Pause.)

Uh-huh.

(Pause.)

Uh-huh.

(Pause.)

Wow. Uh-huh.

(Pause.)

On it. Roger that.

(Pause.)

Sweet dreams.
Over and out.

(Silence.)

So that was Camp Director Linda.
And it appears we have a bit of a...poop situation.
That I have to attend to.

(Pause.)

This was nice. Maybe we can do it again sometime.

(A flash.)

Scene Three

(Several days later. Everyone is looking at their phones. **AIDAN** *stands behind the circle, holding the phone bucket, looking over someone's shoulder. Silence.)*

CASSIE. What're we gonna tell the kids?

(Silence. They all look around at each other. Who's gonna make a call?)

AIDAN. I should walkie Linda.

(He takes a little jog away from the circle to radio Linda.)

Linda, come in.

BECCA. Maybe it's better if we don't tell them. Like, keep camp a safe, sacred space as much as we can?

MAEVE. For sure. The rallies aren't happening here. It doesn't have to be a camp issue.

CASSIE. Aren't they gonna find out at the end of the summer no matter what?

BECCA. Probably yeah.

CASSIE. I just remember a lot of people lied to me a lot when I was a kid? Like, I thought I was a year younger than I was for a long time, because my parents wanted me to think I was a genius. And like, they told me I had a twin sister that I ate in utero, and that whenever I got mad that was her spirit trying to escape my body? And when I found out a lot of that stuff wasn't true eventually I...I guess I had trouble trusting any of those people?

So if they find out, and they know we knew, and didn't tell them, that might affect how much they feel like they can trust us?

MAEVE. *(Deeply concerned.)* You're so right. That, like, can't happen.

(She closes her eyes and starts to think hard. **LUKAS** *is looking at his phone.)*

LUKAS. *(Disgusted, sad.)* Ugh.

BECCA. What?

LUKAS. It's just this video from the Cincinnati Truth Squad rally. A protester threw a piña colada at a Truth Commander, and then the Truth Commander drove his van into the crowd of protesters and a bunch more people died.

CASSIE. Oh god.

MAEVE. Okay...okay! This is a learning opportunity. We bring everyone into the Founders Lodge, we show them the pineapple, we explain what's happening, and break them into discussion groups so they can talk about if they see Dwayne "The Rock" Johnson or not, and how we celebrate those differences in perspective.

BECCA. Yes. That's a really good idea Maeve. And just to piggyback off of that, my only concern is that it might sound like if every perspective is valid then the perspective of "kill protesters" is valid?

MAEVE. That's not what I want.

BECCA. *(Almost cutting her off.)* Exactly. So maybe we let everyone know they're safe here, and make it clear that killing people is morally indefensible no matter what you feel.

MAEVE. I love that. I love that. I love that, and worry a bit that if it's too top-down, it's gonna take away their chance to build confidence in their emotional radar.

BECCA. Of course! I want all our campers to have super strong emotional radars. I just think –

LUKAS. I don't know. I don't know. Maybe we don't need to make it a whole thing. Like, I think we're really underestimating the level of danger and realness these kids are used to dealing with on a daily basis. They know how the world is. Big Chris wrote a poem in his dawn diary about it. It was called "This Is How The World Is." And it's heartbreaking. When he shared it, the other boys snapped so much, because they felt it too.

So like, maybe we just tell them in our own cabins, and they'll absorb it and move on.

(**AIDAN** *comes back.*)

AIDAN. Sorry. What'd I miss?

MAEVE. We were just brainstorming the best way to talk to the kids about what's happening, like, if we gather them all in the Founders Lodge and we / show them –

AIDAN. Oh, we're not gonna tell them about this.

MAEVE. Well, the idea is we show them the pineapple and then break into discussion groups –

AIDAN. We're not showing anyone anything. CDL and I are on the same page about this. It's not necessary and it's not camp appropriate.

MAEVE. Someone needs to explain to them –

AIDAN. Their parents can explain to them however they want, if they want, when the session is over. In the meantime, it's our job to make sure they don't find out about this, and stay focused on activities and personal growth. I understand you're all the real senior counselors and we do really value your input, you know, really look to you as leaders. But in this case we need you to follow.

MAEVE. But they won't trust us. Cassie, you were saying this is gonna affect if they can trust us. Right?

CASSIE. Potentially, but I'll do whatever.

AIDAN. Thank you, Cassie. *(To* **MAEVE.***)* This decision is made. I appreciate your enthusiasm though.

MAEVE. *(Threatening.)* Don't talk to me like that.

AIDAN. Maeve, I am technically your boss. And the part you're not seeing is telling them is just gonna make a mess that you're not responsible for cleaning up.

MAEVE. I am responsible.

AIDAN. Well, I'm sorry that I made you upset. I'm gonna remove myself from the situation.

MAEVE. You're acting like Dad. You look so much like Dad right now.

*(***AIDAN***, stone-faced, slowly turns and goes. As he's leaving, under his breath...)*

AIDAN. Don't stay up too late.

(Silence.)

CASSIE. So we don't tell them.

BECCA. *(Encouraging.)* It's fine! By the end of the summer there'll be some new terrible thing everyone's talking about instead.

LUKAS. I'm really sorry about that, Maeve. And I wanna hold space for your hurt.

(Quiet. **MAEVE** *doesn't say anything.)*

Cool. And now I'd like to hold space for logistically is there anything we have to do to keep this a secret from the kids for the rest of the session? Like, what does this mean for us?

MAEVE. *(Quietly.)* I think it mostly means we just do nothing. None of them have their phones. So it's just business as usual.

LUKAS. Word.

BECCA. Oh my god wait what about Gorgeous Kylie? Didn't her management make a deal with CDL about phone time?

CASSIE. Yeah, but she's super mature about it. She actually told me she wanted to totally unplug, but she's been doing Cameos to raise money for the children's hospital. So it's only like fifteen minutes a day of me shooting her wishing people like, happy birthday.

I think if she found out and we asked her to keep it a secret, she'd be able to do it.

BECCA. I think we have to treat her like everyone else. Even if that's hard sometimes.

LUKAS. Also, Gorgeous Kylie is definitely mature, but she's also nine?

CASSIE. I guess I just don't know how to tell her she can't use her phone without her knowing something's up. Also, her management is very litigious. They've been very clear about that.

BECCA. What if...we tell Kylie that...her management reached out to us and said that the children's hospital is maybe getting canceled for...something? So they want to put a pause on the Cameos.

(She thinks about this.)

Painkillers. They're getting kids hooked on painkillers.

(Everyone processes this.)

CASSIE. I guess that could work.

BECCA. Yeah. I can talk to her at breakfast. We haven't met yet, but like –

LUKAS. I mean, she's Cassie's camper.

CASSIE. Yeah I can tell her. But thanks.

BECCA. Totally. Totally.

(Pause.)

MAEVE. Maybe it doesn't matter if they trust us after this summer, because they're probably never gonna see us again.

(A flash.)

Scene Four

(Several nights later. Everyone but **CASSIE** *is admiring the new plastic bracelets on their wrists.)*

MAEVE. They're so beautiful.

BECCA. Aren't they pretty? I keep telling her mine's so pretty.

CASSIE. We've been doing a whole thing with reclaimed plastic from the ocean. So the plastic you're wearing could've choked a fish. Or a turtle.

LUKAS. Or a shark?

CASSIE. Possibly.

LUKAS. *(Mesmerized.)* Dang.

CASSIE. I picked these out special to match each of your personalities.

(Everyone looks at their wrist, trying to figure out what this means.)

MAEVE. That's...wow. Thank you.

CASSIE. So yeah, these finally arriving was my Oh Yay. Becca?

BECCA. Well, Cassie and I had a super fun day off together... That doesn't count as my Oh Yay.

My No Way is that Cassie was gonna show me her parents' place but they weren't home.

CASSIE. Sorry. They're gone for work a lot. I've given up on keeping track of their schedules.

BECCA. It's so okay. We still got to walk around the house and it was really pretty. It's like this deep deep forest green, with these big panoramic windows facing the lake.

CASSIE. They kind of splurged.

BECCA. *(Secretively.)* They have a boat.

CASSIE. Yeah, they must've just gotten it. They...named it.

BECCA. The Second Chance.

CASSIE. *(To* **BECCA.***)* Do you want to do your Oh Yay?

BECCA. Oh my god I would've forgotten. My Oh Yay is we got a treat for everyone in town.

(She takes out s'mores stuff and passes it around.)

MAEVE. Ooh yum!

LUKAS. Nice.

BECCA. It was crazy. There were all these signs in the produce section about how they don't stock pineapples and please not to bring guns into the store.

LUKAS. Dang.

BECCA. The world is kind of terrible, but I had a pretty good day. *(Remembering* **CASSIE.***)* *We* had a pretty good day. Right?

CASSIE. Yeah. I just feel lucky we're somewhere so remote and like, out of harm's way. *(To* **LUKAS.***)* Can I have a beer?

MAEVE. Yes girl, cut loose!

LUKAS. *(Starting to get one for her.)* You sure it's okay? Like with your meds?

CASSIE. No, they're still missing. The pharmacy has to special order them from Europe. So... *(She cracks open the beer.)* Why not make the most of it, right?

MAEVE. Well it sounds nice. To have your day off with someone cool.

LUKAS. Yeah.

MAEVE. *(To* **LUKAS.***)* When's your day off again?

(**LUKAS** *stares at* **MAEVE.**)

LUKAS. Tuesdays.

(**MAEVE** *stares at* **LUKAS.**)

MAEVE. Maybe I can ask Linda if I can have Tuesdays. Also.

(They both stare at each other.)

LUKAS. Word.

(Weird silence.)

BECCA. Okay, well, I was thinking, I know it's early to plan this, but for our between-session weekend, Cassie, would it be okay, maybe, to ask your parents if we could stay at their place?

CASSIE. Uh –

MAEVE. Ooh yeah that'd be so nice. We'd be really respectful.

CASSIE. I mean...yeah okay I'll ask them. They can be kind of particular about...everything, I guess, and I wouldn't want to stress you all out with a lot of rules about, like, where towels go.

LUKAS. It's okay if not. Maybe we should try to go off the lake anyway. These neighbors, I mean... Cass, I'm sure your parents are dope, but –

CASSIE. They're not.

LUKAS. Okay, but like, yeah. But these neighbors are total narcs. They truly call Sheriff Jablonski if a kid, like, sneezes.

MAEVE. We're lucky he's wet for Linda.

CASSIE. Off the lake could be nice. How was everything here? What'd we miss?

MAEVE. We had a really special day. Lukas and I surprised our bunks by waking them up at sunrise, and we did the Whisper Walk up Caroline Creek.

BECCA. Whoa. I must've slept through that.

MAEVE. I made sure everyone stayed quiet so we wouldn't wake you on your day off.

(To **CASSIE.***)* You have to go at dawn and walk so quietly and whisper because that's when all the animals go to the creek to drink. And if you're really lucky. You can see something special.

BECCA. Were you?

MAEVE. What?

BECCA. Really lucky?

*(***MAEVE** *slowly smiles.)*

MAEVE. *(Whispered.)* A caribou family.

BECCA. *(Quiet disbelief.)* What.

MAEVE. *(Whispered.)* A whole family. Of caribou.

LUKAS. *(Also whispering for some reason.)* And then we went to the mess early and New Chef Michelle made us Early Breakfast. Pancakes. And hot chocolate. With whipped cream. On everything.

It felt like one of those days. That the campers are never gonna forget.

BECCA. Wow. I just wish I'd known you guys were planning something like that.

MAEVE. Oh, yeah, it kind of just happened?

BECCA. That's...incredible. For that to just happen.

MAEVE. Well, we talked about it before, when I was walking Lukas back to his cabin last night.

LUKAS. I'm not embarrassed to say, the path behind the boathouse is too dark and scary for me.

MAEVE. But the topic came up super spontaneously, I meant. We weren't trying to leave anyone out of anything.

CASSIE. Well it sounds really special.

BECCA. It really does. Sound really special.

*(**AIDAN** enters, visibly exhausted, carrying the phone bucket and a big thermos of coffee.)*

AIDAN. Phones.

(He starts to pass out everyone's phones.)

Can't stay and chat tonight, I'm afraid. Gotta keep moving. Lots to do, lots to do.

(He takes a sip from his thermos. He does not enjoy it.)

LUKAS. Is that coffee?

AIDAN. Gotta keep my senses sharp. Eyes. Ears. Smelling, maybe. It's gonna be another late, late night.

LUKAS. I just thought caffeine...

AIDAN. *(Kind of losing it.)* Well, we all have to make sacrifices sometimes!

MAEVE. Did you...not sleep?

AIDAN. *(Through a yawn.)* Not so much. But I'm okay.

MAEVE. Why?

AIDAN. You don't have to worry about it. Besides, I had a lot to keep me busy. Linda's been having to deal with all these city council meetings with the neighbors, so I'm picking up the slack. The thought of her sitting behind that table with that little microphone and being yelled at by neighbor after neighbor... They want all these ordinances passed about splashing. So –

(He's cut off by a sharp pain in his stomach. He stands still and groans a strange groan. They all stare.)

LUKAS. Are you okay?

AIDAN. *(Through pain, still groaning.)* It's just the coffee.

BECCA. *(Worried about his pain.)* Do you want to sit down for a second?

AIDAN. *(Sitting, not really thinking about it.)* For a second, for a second.

(He's seated, and the pain subsides. But then he looks around and realizes he's part of the group. He did it. He smiles.)

Well.

Well well well. Here we are.

You know, I know you all think of me as your boss, but I want you to think of me as your mentor.

You can come to me with anything.

BECCA. Okay. Why aren't you sleeping?

AIDAN. *(Hedging.)* Well –

CASSIE. You said we could come to you with anything.

(Pause. **AIDAN***'s caught. He thinks, and makes a decision.)*

AIDAN. I'm keeping watch. Last night, some campers saw something...someone...in the woods.

(A flash.)

Scene Five

(Several days later. The **COUNSELORS** *are editing letters that have arrived from campers' parents.)*

CASSIE. Okay, I'm stuck on "A lot of our neighbors have joined the Truth Militias, and they're trying hard to get us to too, but we don't believe in what they're fighting for."

MAEVE. Joined the Truth...Community?

CASSIE. I think that might sound like a cult.

MAEVE. It's not a cult, it's a community.

CASSIE. That's what a cult would say.

BECCA. How about "book clubs"?

CASSIE. *(Reading to herself.)* A lot of our neighbors have joined the book clubs, and they're trying hard to get us to too, but we don't believe in what they're...reading about.

Okay, that works!

LUKAS. I think we have to throw out Timothy's letter again.

MAEVE. No!

CASSIE. There's gotta be something salvageable in there. It's worse for him to get nothing, right?

LUKAS. I guess?

"We have risen through the ranks of the *book club*. We are amassing *books* for our arsenal and now the *bookstores* are almost empty, so we are well-equipped to defend our right to *drink wine and mingle.* When the final *book club meeting* comes we will rain down *literacy* upon our –"

CASSIE. Yeah no throw it away.

LUKAS. Timothy knows something's up. When his parents dropped him off they said they'd write to him every day. Now he wants us to do our Rainbow Summit presentation about the power of a broken promise.

CASSIE. That actually reminds me of a question. So, I might have spaced on this or missed it somehow, but I was working more with my cabin on our presentation for Rainbow Summit, and I know we have to do a presentation, and make an offering, and wear a color. But what actually is the Rainbow Summit supposed to be?

(Quiet. Everyone thinks about this.)

Like, I guess I don't know what we're supposed to be preparing for.

MAEVE. You can prepare your spirit?

AIDAN. It's a celebration of community, cooperation –

CASSIE. No, I understand that part. I guess my question was more about what activities we were planning to do.

BECCA. Well I think we kind of figured by the time everyone finished their offerings and presentations it'd basically be time for dinner.

CASSIE. Hm. Okay. I think I'm confused about what Rainbow Summit's trying to do other than not be bad?

AIDAN. Let's not discount the value of not being bad.

CASSIE. But like are there goals?

MAEVE. To not be competitive and collectively contribute to camp culture?

(She thinks.)

I guess I don't know how the presentations and offerings do that exactly, but –

CASSIE. So I actually had a thought about that. We do an exercise in Junior Diplomats about collective problem-solving called Roundtable Relay, which we could try with real camp issues? So, each cabin can bring an issue they've noticed, and we'll all work together to solve them.

BECCA. *(Doing her best to hide that she does not want to try this.)* Oh wow! That sounds... That's really interesting! Like –

LUKAS. Can you show us? How it would work? I think I'm just having trouble imagining.

CASSIE. Okay, sure.

BECCA. Demonstration!!

CASSIE. *(To herself.)* How do I do this?

(Now out loud.) Okay! Point of order. The Cassie Delegation requests the floor?

(She looks at them expectantly.)

You have to grant me the floor.

(They don't know how to grant her the floor.)

Just say, "The floor is granted."

ALL. *(Variously.)* The floor is granted.

CASSIE. *(Comfy, almost casual with the jargon.)* The People of Cassie bring a concern to the Committee of... Senior Counselors.

MAEVE. Woo!

CASSIE. Activities sign-up is currently first come, first serve. This is a broken system. I propose –

BECCA. Wait I'm confused, is this like a silly example problem or are you saying this for real?

CASSIE. Well, I'm saying it as an example, but I also think it's real, right?

(Pause.)

BECCA. It's first come first serve.

CASSIE. Yes, which creates some problems with fairness.

AIDAN. Really? I feel like the first come, first serve system is all about fairness. You know, anyone can come first, and be served first, and that can change any day. Every day is full of possibility.

MAEVE. It is such an amazing rush to like, get to the mess and realize you're first.

CASSIE. I'm sure it is. But I know at least my cabin hasn't gotten to be first yet.

MAEVE. Oh my god but when you do it's gonna feel amazing I promise!

CASSIE. I think the thing I'm realizing is different groups of campers need different amounts of time and attention to get ready in the morning. Like, my campers, who are all eight- and nine-year-old girls, take a lot of time to get washed up and get dressed and ready, but it seems like it must be faster for boy cabins, because they get more early sign-ups. And my campers need a lot of help with things, like drying their hair and making their beds, because they're younger, so even when a girls cabin gets an early sign-up, they tend to be the older girls, because they're more self-sufficient, so one of the counselors can run ahead.

MAEVE. *(A bit oblivious.)* Oh yeah I do that.

CASSIE. Right. So basically, in the current system, a cabin like Lukas's has a much better chance of getting its first pick of activities than a cabin like mine.

LUKAS. Yeah, I mean, I definitely have felt lucky this year. And I can for sure see how that's related to the campers that I have. But I've tried to be mindful of that, and rotate what activities I pick, so we're not, like, hogging all the good ones.

MAEVE. That's so thoughtful.

CASSIE. And we're lucky to have someone in your position like you, Lukas, who's already thinking about fairness. But even then, like...so there are only enough boating slots for each cabin to go twice per session, right? But Lukas's cabin has already had three boating sessions.

LUKAS. *(Really struck by this.)* Whoa. I mean, I guess... Anthony A. was sick the first time, and he loves the kayak, and then the twins did an Above and Beyond and so we wanted to reward them for that, and... I'm sorry. I'm sorry.

CASSIE. It's okay. It shouldn't be on one person to always have to do the right thing. We just need a better system.

LUKAS. *(Breaking down.)* I'm sorry. I'm sorry everyone. I've let you down. We'll never boat again.

(He begins to violently, rhythmically hit himself in the head.)

CASSIE. That's really not what I'm saying.

MAEVE. I just wanna take a moment to say that if this is making Lukas feel this way, I don't know if it's a good idea to do with campers.

CASSIE. Yeah, maybe not I guess.

AIDAN. I don't think the activity is what's making Lukas feel bad.

MAEVE. Then what's making him feel bad?

AIDAN. I think Lukas went boating too many times, and somebody noticed.

(Pause.)

MAEVE. *(Quietly, to* **CASSIE.***)* So now what do we do?

CASSIE. *(Regrouping.)* Okay. Well, no one is allowed to bring a concern to the floor without bringing a proposed solution. I brought the concern, so my solution is: a lottery.

BECCA. Um, okay. Interesting. I see a few problems. Like –

CASSIE. Great! Okay, Becca, that is one hundred percent the next step. Critical questioning. It's just not quite your turn yet. This is a roundtable so we always go around clockwise, which means it's Aidan's turn.

AIDAN. So I'm supposed to critically question the lottery idea?

CASSIE. Yes.

AIDAN. *(Pleasantly surprised to be included.)* Well. Let's see.

(He thinks.)

A lottery system is like gambling. Which we shouldn't encourage the kids to do. Also, it's pure chance. It's chaos. It's meaningless. Nothing means anything. You could do gimp twelve days in a row. Why? No reason. It's just your fate. Handed down to you by a cruel god. Or you could do archery every day, but was it because you showed initiative and showed up early? No, because to reiterate, nothing means anything. Bleep bloop blorp everything is goo running on electricity. Great lesson for the kids. Nothing you do changes anything!

CASSIE. Great. So now you propose a solution to *that* problem.

AIDAN. My solution is...we go back to the first come, first serve sign-up.

CASSIE. Okay. That's called a regression, and would lose you points, if we were doing this for points, but we're not! Your solution should refine, not replace. What's the solution to a lottery being more fair, but too random?

AIDAN. *(Really thinking.)* Hmmm. Hmmmmm. Maybe... instead of assigning activities randomly, we can assign them based on a predetermined, scheduled rotation. That way we have structure. And rules. That we can all understand.

CASSIE. Amazing. That makes a lot of sense. Becca, I know you've got this. It's your turn. The floor is yours.

BECCA. The problem with a scheduled rotation? So I want to zoom out and examine the overall assumption that like, certain activities are inherently more desirable than others? We have a lot of incredible specialists at this camp and there's kind of an insulting insinuation in some of this that, like, pottery with Art Stacy isn't fun. It's...so fun. I keep my toothbrush in my pinch pot. All of our activities are special. Everyone should want to do all of our activities.

MAEVE. *(Confused.)* But we haven't done pottery this year.

BECCA. Because we didn't have to, but if we did, it would be so much fun.

LUKAS. We should be honest, there is a hierarchy. There is.

BECCA. *(Losing patience.)* Well even if there is, it's not wrong that older kids get to do more of the high-demand activities. For a young camper, Nature Nick's porcupine presentation is educational, funny as heck, and the porcupine itself is a thing of wonder. But your fourth or fifth summer, you've seen the porcupine. So a certain level of seniority in picking activities actually helps everyone do the right thing for them.

CASSIE. Okay. Propose your solution.

BECCA. That fixes all of that?

CASSIE. Or as much as you can. Other people will fix the pieces you can't figure out.

BECCA. No, I want to try.

(She thinks seriously.)

BECCA. What if?! We can do trades! We have a rotation system, but counselors can trade activities among themselves so everyone gets what's best for them that day, or at least close.

CASSIE. Becca! Incredible! Lukas?

LUKAS. I'm really just trying to take a step back to listen and reflect.

CASSIE. Okay. And part of listening can be contributing.

LUKAS. Listening...to myself.

A problem I think I would run into, personally, with trades, if I'm being brutally real with all of you, is that I like you guys. More than younger counselors I don't know as well. And I'm afraid that I would unconsciously be more likely to trade activities with one of you than with someone else. And we cannot rely on individuals to do the right thing. I learned that the hard way.

CASSIE. So...

LUKAS. My solution. That I propose...

Is anonymous swaps. There's a bulletin board in the mess, and you can post a request for a swap on a notecard, and then someone with the activity you want can choose to accept. But you don't know who each other is! That's the beauty of it. You swap for the activity. Not the counselor.

CASSIE. Maeve!

MAEVE. *(Overwhelmed.)* Ahhhhhh ummmmmmmm wow! Wow wow wow! I think... I just love everyone's contributions so much and everyone's thoughtfulness and I think I'm just feeling overwhelmed? Like, confused? Because first come first serve was so straightforward and now there's a schedule, but it's not your schedule, 'cause you can trade your schedule, but in the mess like the first come first serve sign-ups? And are the trades first come first serve? Or does that just create the same problem and it never ever goes away? And I just feel I just feel I just feel...it's a lot.

BECCA. That's a good point. Are we making something too confusing?

LUKAS. *(To* **MAEVE.***)* So if it's too confusing what's the solution?

MAEVE. I don't know!

LUKAS. You got this.

MAEVE. I don't!

LUKAS. You do.

MAEVE. But it's confusing!

LUKAS. Make it not confusing.

*(***MAEVE** *thinks. Then.)*

MAEVE. I don't wanna take away everyone's good ideas, and I'm worried this might do that.

But.

What if instead of rotating activities, we have rotating assigned choice order? So every bunk gets to choose activities first and last the same amount? People can pick what's right for them, but it's fair, and no swaps, sorry Lukas and Becca I think swaps are good they just confuse me.

(Pause.)

That's it.

CASSIE. That's a great idea Maeve. I don't see a problem with it I can solve. Do any other delegates have remaining concerns? And you say yea or nay.

ALL BUT CASSIE. *(Variously.)* Nay. / ? / !

CASSIE. Amazing! Then I'll move to close the floor. Does anybody second the motion?

BECCA. I do! I second the motion.

CASSIE. Which brings us to a vote. Shall we close the floor? Yea or nay?

ALL BUT CASSIE. Yea.

CASSIE. The motion passes, the concern is resolved, the floor is closed. And then I would bang my gavel but I don't have one right now. And that's how it works. So we came to a good solution we can all agree on, and we can put it in place as soon as tomorrow.

LUKAS. Wait, like, for real?

CASSIE. For real.

(Silence. Everyone looks at each other.)

BECCA. Maybe we should think on it? Let the idea marinate for a bit.

AIDAN. Also, I'd have to ask CDL, and she's dealing with a lot right now. Maybe it's something we can consider for next session.

MAEVE. Yeah it might be too confusing to switch systems mid-session.

CASSIE. Okay.

LUKAS. *(Kind of consoling* **CASSIE.***)* But we can definitely keep it in mind as a possibility for next session.

CASSIE. Cool. I guess it's just a question of what you care about more. Taking the best care of these kids that you can? Or doing things the way you've always done them.

AIDAN. We're not saying we don't want to, we're just saying it's not easy to –

CASSIE. *(Frustrated.)* If a sign-up sheet isn't easy I don't know what we're ever gonna be able to do about things that are hard.

(Pause.)

But yeah, that wasn't even really the point, I guess. I just think the exercise could give Rainbow Summit some structure. And purpose.

BECCA. Yeah, totally. Yeah.

LUKAS. I can see that.

MAEVE. I don't know. I think...it's a lot of new special lingo. Like, "the floor"...? Which maybe is alienating. And if the point is to make everyone feel like part of the community, and not be competitive, I just don't want to exclude people because we didn't think it through. But thank you Cassie.

CASSIE. Who are we excluding?

LUKAS. Yeah, I guess I don't totally understand.

MAEVE. Like, kids who don't feel good at stuff like Roundtable Relay.

AIDAN. *(Confused.)* So does soccer exclude the kids who aren't good at soccer? That's not good.

MAEVE. That's not what I mean. I mean, like, like, Becca, like, you struggled with this, right? And like, Lukas, it seems like it brought up some stuff that was really difficult for you? So like –

LUKAS. Oh, but I'm excited to try Roundtable Relay with the kids.

BECCA. Yeah, it was tough, but I liked it.

MAEVE. Well then I guess, I guess, like, like, like, like, like... I guess then it's just me but it made me feel really bad. Yeah. And stupid, and small. And it just kept going around and around and I couldn't stop it and I couldn't, I couldn't...and what about the kids like me? What about the kids like me?

CASSIE. Well what about the kids like me?

(Silence.)

MAEVE. That's not what I –

That's not, I would never, like –

I have to go to the bathroom.

I've really been hydrating a lot and I need to go to the bathroom right now.

Lukas will you come with me?

LUKAS. Uh...okay. Yeah.

*(**MAEVE** leaves quickly, with **LUKAS** close behind.)*

AIDAN. Cassie, I have to say, you've really impressed me tonight. At this rate, by next summer, you could be up for assistant assistant camp director. It's not an official position yet. But I've been thinking about it a lot.

CASSIE. Thanks.

AIDAN. Maybe we could Roundtable Relay the idea!

CASSIE. Yeah. Maybe. It seems like Roundtable Relay might not really be the vibe.

BECCA. I'm so sorry about Maeve's attitude. She shouldn't get to act like that.

CASSIE. It's fine.

BECCA. No! Like, listen. The thing you have to understand is, Maeve is like my closest friend. I love her so much. So much it hurts. And we've known each other so long, and there's all this history, and she's so special in so many ways and she's smart and thoughtful and intuitive and fun and she knows me better than anyone, and I know her better than anyone, and that's a bond you can't break, you know? That's a bond you can't break. And she's pretty. Right? She's so pretty. And cool and awesome and has so much love to give.

And so I say this with love, and respect, but also honesty, because I think that's what Maeve would most especially want: having her as a co has been a little bit tough sometimes.

And I'm not perfect. I'm really not. But I always try to be better. And sometimes it seems like Maeve isn't trying. And I get that because in a lot of ways Maeve doesn't need to change. But she has a way of doing things? And it's her way? And that's a really fun way but sometimes it's not the most responsible way? I mean, she's a great counselor. Everyone's always saying, "Maeve, you're the best counselor." But I think what I'm realizing, because I've never worked this closely with her before this summer, is being "the best counselor" doesn't always mean being the best counselor? If that makes sense?

CASSIE. I think?

BECCA. Like you brought up activities. Sometimes Maeve just...disappears during our activities. And I don't know where she is. And all our girls will be like, "Where's Maeve? We want Maeve!" And I'm like, so do I, you know? And I end up just feeling really alone.

I'm sorry if that's weird to hear, Aidan. I do love her.

AIDAN. No, I get it. I get it.

Well, I'm off to start the rounds. Another night to –

(His knees buckle and he falls.)

CASSIE. Whoa.

BECCA. Hey, I think you need to get some sleep.

AIDAN. Someone has to stay up in case –

CASSIE. Aidan, you haven't seen anything, right?

AIDAN. Right.

CASSIE. So maybe it worked. Maybe whoever it was is scared off and it's over. And now you're more valuable to camp with a good night's sleep than...like this. Okay? We need you. Right?

BECCA. Yeah.

AIDAN. Okay. Okay I'll sleep.

Don't stay up too late.

*(**AIDAN** leaves and passes **LUKAS** and **MAEVE** as they re-enter. **MAEVE** is bashful.)*

MAEVE. We're back!

(Pause. They sit.)

I'm excited. To do Roundtable Relay.

CASSIE. Not everyone has to be excited about every single activity.

MAEVE. No I am. I wasn't seeing it clearly before but I am more now, and I think it's important.

CASSIE. It's just a game.

MAEVE. But the kids should get used to things changing. To changing things.

I'm sorry.

I really want you to like it here.

*(Silence. Suddenly, all of their phones start buzzing at the same time. An emergency notification. **LUKAS** looks at his phone. Others follow.)*

LUKAS. Oh shit.

CASSIE. NCA. I mean, what?

LUKAS. I think they just took Kansas.

(They all look at each other. A flash.)

Scene Six

(Several days later. The group is deep in a brainstorming session.)

CASSIE. I don't really see how we can have a drill if we don't tell the kids what we're doing a drill for.

MAEVE. We could make it like a game? Like a camp-wide game of hide-and-seek that can start at any moment.

LUKAS. Some of them aren't very good at hiding.

CASSIE. And they still wouldn't have any reason to take this that seriously.

MAEVE. Like, maybe we could offer them a really amazing prize for whoever's found last? Prizes are good motivators. Like, a popsicle.

BECCA. I'm just worried about sending everyone off to hide on their own. Like, Lukas is right that some of the kids are really bad hiders. But we haven't even thought about the kids who are really good hiders. They can fit anywhere. And when this whole game drill thing is over we're gonna have to find them, and if they're motivated to stay hidden… I don't know. I don't know.

*(**AIDAN** jogs in.)*

AIDAN. Well, that's the last of the early pick-ups. The kids are all excited for their "surprise family vacations." I just hope the drive back is safe with all the new checkpoints.

CASSIE. I'm surprised so many people aren't doing early pick-up.

BECCA. Yeah, I think a lot of them think it's safer here.

AIDAN. Oh, and I went back out around the lake to check in with the neighbors, and none of them say they've seen anyone walking by their places at night. But I don't think we can trust them. I think it must've been one of them.

CASSIE. Maybe it was a camper playing a prank? A really confusing prank?

AIDAN. *(Showing her a picture on his phone.)* This doesn't look like a prank to me. Piling all our firewood around the chair shed like that? To me it looks like someone building a bonfire. It looks like a threat.

MAEVE. *(Who's been thinking about her idea.)* It could be *group* hide-and-seek.

AIDAN. What?

BECCA. We were trying to think of some drill to get the kids out of sight quickly.

AIDAN. You think they're surveilling this far out already?

CASSIE. They said something on their podcast about wanting to be bicoastal.

LUKAS. You think the chair shed could've been a Truth Squad thing? Like, I don't know what it symbolizes, but we don't know these neighbors' politics.

MAEVE. So if it's group hide-and-seek, everyone hears an announcement on the intercom, like a code word –

AIDAN. Falcon.

MAEVE. So the kids hear "Falcon," run to their bunks, we get a head count, and then we hide together.

LUKAS. And then whichever cabin stays hidden longest gets a popsicle party!

BECCA. If all the kids are hiding together in their bunks, like, they're gonna know we know where they're hidden. I don't think they'll think it's a game. I don't know if a game is even the responsible way to go.

CASSIE. We could still tell the kids what's going on. If that's gonna help keep everyone safer.

AIDAN. I don't know. The second we tell the kids, this isn't camp anymore. It becomes something really different, that none of us know how to handle.

MAEVE. Okay okay okay! It's group hide-and-seek –

BECCA. *(Interrupting.)* Maeve...

MAEVE. But! We can have challenges they have to do when they get back to the bunk! Like, a puzzle, or a craft. And they have to do it together, silently. Near the floor, below the windows. And whoever finishes first wins. No, whoever finishes best wins. We might need it to take a while.

BECCA. If the cabins are all competing against each other, that's just doing the same thing we're trying to stop doing with Rainbow Summit.

MAEVE. Everyone's craft can be part of one big craft. And when we're done hiding slash crafting, we can all come together in the Founders Lodge and put the craft together. And if CDL thinks it's good enough –

AIDAN. If it captures the spirit of camp!

MAEVE. – then she can decide that everyone gets popsicles.

(Pause.)

BECCA. That's...wow, that's really smart Maeve. I think it's a super creative way to take care of the kids. And keep them safe. I wasn't trying to be negative.

MAEVE. *(Sincere.)* Thank you, Becca. That actually means a lot. I know I'm not always the easiest person to work with.

BECCA. What? What're you talking about?

MAEVE. I mean sometimes we have different ideas about how to do things, and I don't want that to be a burden on you. I want you to have an amazing summer.

BECCA. *(Confused.)* I'm having an amazing summer.

MAEVE. And I don't want to get in the way of that. So if it'd be better for you, Cassie and I talked, and you two could switch bunks. I'd understand.

BECCA. I don't want that.

MAEVE. You'd get to be with Gorgeous Kylie.

And Cassie, you're always saying Rachel is a really awesome co.

BECCA. *(Frozen, quiet.)* I don't want to be cos with Rachel. I want to be cos with you.

MAEVE. Are you sure?

BECCA. Yeah.

MAEVE. *(Somehow terrifying.)* Are you really sure?

BECCA. Yes, Maeve.

MAEVE. Good. I'm glad.

*(**BECCA** looks down and gets on her phone.)*

Aidan, do you want to check with Linda to see if this drill works for her?

AIDAN. Right. Yeah, yeah. I'll do that.

(Into his radio.) Linda, come in.

(He walks into the corner to talk to Linda.)

CASSIE. Should we also maybe do some more survival-training sessions?

LUKAS. Oh yeah I could use a brush-up on my first aid. And orienteering.

MAEVE. But for like, a worst-case scenario, right?

LUKAS. I mean, all this training is always for a worst-case scenario.

CASSIE. Yeah, I meant for the campers, but we could all do it too.

MAEVE. Maybe we can find a way to subtly incorporate it into their activities.

AIDAN. *(Returning.)* We got the all clear from CDL! Good work team. I'll get popsicles in the morning.

CASSIE. Cool. We should all get some sleep.

AIDAN. You all go ahead. I have to keep watch again. Whoever set up that bonfire around the chair shed could still be out there.

CASSIE. No, you've already done so many nights. I can do it.

MAEVE. Above and beyond, Cassie.

LUKAS. Yeah thank you Cassie. Above and beyond.

BECCA. I'll stay up with you.

CASSIE. I'm really fine.

BECCA. No. No one should have to keep watch alone. I'll stay.

AIDAN. That's smart. It's probably a good idea for the time being to have an overnight watch. We'll do it in pairs. I'll set up a chart!

(He starts to go, excited to set up a chart.)

CASSIE. *(Calling after him.)* In the morning, Aidan.

AIDAN. *(Pausing.)* In the morning.

*(***AIDAN, MAEVE,** *and* **LUKAS** *leave.)*

CASSIE. I'm really fine on my own. If you want to go to bed.

BECCA. No I wanna stay.

(Quiet.)

CASSIE. Did you notice the –

BECCA. *(Even.)* So you and Maeve talked.

CASSIE. Yeah.

BECCA. That's cool. It's cool to see you guys getting closer.

I guess... I'm just trying to understand what you two were talking about? Like, in terms of me.

CASSIE. In what sense?

BECCA. In whatever sense you like.

(Pause.)

CASSIE. I just mentioned that you had some concerns about how you two were working together.

BECCA. *(Eerily level.)* And why would you do that?

*(***CASSIE*** doesn't answer, slightly surprised.* ***BECCA*** *continues.)*

I'm just trying to understand why something I said to you in confidence would randomly come up in front of my friend. Because, as far as I know you, Cassie, you're a kind person. And you're smart. And you pick up on social cues. So it's hard for me to imagine you didn't realize that that wasn't something for you to just say, you know?

And so then it's like why. Why would you say that? I know it must be hard to be new, and not know anyone, or how anything works. So maybe that's it?

And clearly you're so accomplished, with the bracelets and school and everything, and to come here where everything's different and none of that stuff really matters, that must be destabilizing. To not really know who you are here.

I've really tried to be kind to you, and welcoming. So I really just wanna know.

Why are you trying to ruin my life?

CASSIE. You told me you felt alone.

And it seemed like you didn't realize things don't have to be that way.

I was trying to help.

BECCA. Well you really helped.

CASSIE. And maybe it can change now. Now that she knows.

BECCA. *(Angry, embarrassed.)* I don't want it to change. I've learned to live with the way it is, okay? I understand it.

I don't know if this seems like a game to you, but this is my real life. And in a couple months you're gonna get to go back to your bracelets and school and skiing and whateverthefuck, and I'm still gonna be living in it.

CASSIE. How long?

(Something has shifted. We haven't seen **CASSIE** *like this.)*

BECCA. What?

CASSIE. How long do I have to be here before I'm not a visitor? I've tried to learn all your rules and songs and games. I've tried to make them better. I've tried to go out of my way to prove I care. What is it gonna take for you to let me in?

BECCA. *(Frustrated with how hard this is to figure out.)* I... I... I...like...I don't know, like...go back in time I guess to when you were seven, and convince your parents to send you here, and keep coming back, and live through everything...like, like...

CASSIE. You're saying it's impossible.

BECCA. *(Still frustrated.)* No I'm saying...what I'm saying is you can't ignore that all that history matters...and... and...you're right I am saying it's impossible but that can't be right, so I don't know what is. I don't know.

(Realizing.) I think I'd have to give up something really...

(She makes an aggressive gesture toward her heart with her hand, because she can't think of a better way to explain it.)

And, and I don't know if I'm good enough or strong enough to do it.

CASSIE. Well then maybe I should just go home, right?

BECCA. *(Taken aback.)* What?

CASSIE. Half the kids in my cabin got picked up, so no one actually needs me to be here. There are a lot of good, logical reasons I should go home. And being here just means making the decision to stay again and again and again and I'm really tired. So. Should I go home?

*(**BECCA** tries but can't answer.)*

You can go to bed. I've got this.

BECCA. I'm not gonna make you stay up alone.

CASSIE. Okay. Then I'm gonna go make us some coffee.

(She gets up to go.)

BECCA. *(Calling after her.)* Have you made peace with the way you are?

CASSIE. What?

BECCA. When you did the Questions.

CASSIE. Oh. Not yet, I guess.

BECCA. Maybe that's why you don't want to leave.

(Flash.)

Scene Seven

(Several nights later. **MAEVE** *and* **LUKAS** *sitting with headlamps and a thermos. They've been making the rounds.)*

MAEVE. Have you talked to Shannon recently?

LUKAS. I mean, yeah, why?

MAEVE. Is she like...a Pineapple Person?

LUKAS. No, I mean, I don't think so. Her dad's in the squad, so she reposts his memes, but I think she feels like she has to to be supportive.

MAEVE. Well she's reeeally being supportive.

LUKAS. I don't know what to tell you.

MAEVE. You don't have to, like, defend your ex.

LUKAS. Okay.

(He tries to pour himself more coffee from the thermos.)

Oh dang. I killed the coffee. It was nice of Cassie to make it for us, even when it's not –

MAEVE. *(Interrupting.)* Do you think I'm good at anything?

LUKAS. Like...sexually?

MAEVE. No. Like real things.

LUKAS. I mean, you're an amazing counselor. Obviously.

MAEVE. No. Like real things.

(Pause.)

LUKAS. I guess I mainly know you as a counselor.

MAEVE. Yeah, and not a lot of people are ever going to know me like that.

LUKAS. Well like, all your campers. And then when those campers become counselors, their campers will, like, *(Putting a hand on his chest.) know* you.

MAEVE. So does that mean I've already done the most meaningful thing I'll ever be able to do? Because that makes me feel really old. And embarrassed.

LUKAS. So. What would you tell a camper, if she told you she was feeling this way?

MAEVE. I wouldn't let a camper feel this way.

LUKAS. But if you couldn't stop it. And she did.

(Pause.)

MAEVE. *(Sad but really trying.)* I'd say, "Hey girlfriend, can you imagine a blue tiger?" And she'd say yes. And I'd say, "Have you ever seen a blue tiger?" And she'd say no. And I'd say, "So what's stopping you from imagining better things for yourself just because you haven't seen them yet?"

*(**LUKAS** shrugs.)*

What's your higher purpose?

LUKAS. Huh?

MAEVE. You said something a while ago about a prophecy? And waking up?

LUKAS. Oh that? Uhhhh...

Okay...

So I've been having this dream,

and it's me walking in the woods,

on a beautiful day,

and then there's a clearing,

and in the clearing is a beast.

And it's one of those beasts that's made of a lot of different animals,

like it has the talons of an eagle and the tail of a lion, but I can never see the whole beast. It's too big. I can only look at one part at a time. But it's beautiful.
And the beast speaks to me and says,
"Lo, Lukas,
Hear me.
You are chosen.
Of all my children,
You are blessed with a higher purpose.
You are the bearer of a sacred prophecy that shall be sealed in flame.
I anoint you."
And it touches my face with its wing.
"Go forth, Lukas.
There is much work to be done."
And I'm like, "Do you have any more details?"
And the beast does not,
because it's turned into a pillar of stone.
And the pillar of stone starts to rumble
and crack.
And it etches writing into its own side.
And I take a step towards it.
And that step wakes me up.

Which is kind of a bummer.

MAEVE. Yeah.

LUKAS. And then for the rest of the day, everything I do, I'm like,
"Is this my higher purpose?"
"Is *this* my higher purpose?"

MAEVE. How often do you have the dream?

LUKAS. Ohh, only once or twice a night.

And I keep trying to burn prophecies, but I always freak out halfway because what if I'm right?

MAEVE. It sounds like a lot of responsibility.

LUKAS. And it's like, why me?

I'm just Lukas.

I don't want to be in...a bible.

But I guess at the end of the day, I don't have a choice.

Because the dream is getting louder.

And the beast is getting angrier.

MAEVE. Do you think we're gonna be okay?

Do you think this is gonna get better?

(Pause.)

LUKAS. I think it's gonna get...different.

(Flash.)

Scene Eight

*(**AIDAN** sits. **BECCA** is holding the thermos that Lukas was using.)*

BECCA. Do you want more coffee?

AIDAN. *(Shaking his head.)* It's stopped working for me.

BECCA. Yeah, me too. I don't have the heart to tell Cassie. She's just trying to help.

(Pause.)

The kids know something's wrong, right? They must know.

AIDAN. I don't know. We're the ones who really see the changes. For them it's just how things are.

BECCA. But like, if I were building shelters in arts & crafts, and having to practice covering my tracks on nature walks, and everyone was suddenly taking archery, like, really seriously, I think some part of me would know.

AIDAN. I really think they believe we're preparing for the Super-Secret Ultimate Overnight Hike-A-Thon. If they have to go. If they get to go.

BECCA. I guess I just wonder if we, like, took all the energy we're using to keep them from knowing what's happening, and used it to actually prepare them for if it comes. Would they be better off?

AIDAN. If the campers get to go on the Super-Secret Ultimate Overnight Hike-A-Thon, I think nothing we can say or do will prepare them. Not really.

BECCA. Yeah.

(Silence.)

AIDAN. Thank you for coming back this year. I, uh... I know you didn't want to and you didn't have to, but I think it's meant a lot for Maeve.

BECCA. I'm glad you called me. She, like, told me, obviously, but I don't think I totally registered how bad it was.

AIDAN. She acts like she likes to talk about it, but I don't really think she likes to talk about it.

BECCA. Yeah.

AIDAN. But I'm sorry you have to deal with all of this now.

BECCA. You mean Maeve, or...

AIDAN. I guess all of it.

BECCA. I mean, if I'd been in New York, I'd probably be less safe, so in some ways it's for the best. And there will be other internships.

AIDAN. Probably not at a newspaper, though.

BECCA. Yeah. Probably not.

(Silence. **AIDAN** *reaches into his pocket, takes out an Appreciation sticker, walks over to* **BECCA**, *and puts it on her sleeve.)*

Thank you.

AIDAN. Thank *you.*

(A buzzing noise from above. They notice silently. They look up. A small, flying object passes overhead and then flies low into the area around the campfire. It floats close to **BECCA** *and* **AIDAN** *for a while, looking at them, and then flies away. Silence. They slowly look at each other.)*

Falcon.

(Flash.)

Scene Nine

(Everyone re-enters, decked out in their Rainbow Summit colors, face paint, etc. Things went well today.)

LUKAS. I'll admit it, I had my doubts, but I love a chance to be proven wrong.

MAEVE. I'm really glad we didn't cancel. Like, I didn't know if, like –

CASSIE. Me neither! If I'm being totally honest. I know I was pushing for it, but –

BECCA. It's good that you did! It's so good that you did. The campers needed a change of pace. You could feel it in the room.

CASSIE. *(To* **BECCA** *and* **MAEVE.***)* You guys killed it on your presentaysh.

MAEVE. It was all Becca.

BECCA. We did it together.

MAEVE. *(Sincere.)* Love you, Becca.

(**BECCA** *smiles.)*

AIDAN. And Cassie, I mean, wow. Roundtable Relay? Chills.

CASSIE. Me too.

MAEVE. I just wish CDL could've been there to see it.

BECCA. Oh! I should send her my minutes, right Aidan?

AIDAN. Yeah. Yeah. Thanks.

(**BECCA** *takes out her phone to send the minutes.)*

MAEVE. But she would've loved this.

AIDAN. If she could have seen the kids today. See who they're becoming?

MAEVE. They're gonna be counselors one day.

LUKAS. They're gonna be in charge of everything one day.

(Pause.)

BECCA. Um, hey, no one gave Gorgeous Kylie back her phone, right?

CASSIE. I'm pretty sure not. Why?

BECCA. She's tweeting. She's been tweeting.

CASSIE. You can schedule tweets, / I think.

BECCA. No, but like, it's about the Truth Squad. It's about the pineapple.

(Everyone freezes.)

She wants to get the hashtag "peace is gorgeous" trending.

*(***CASSIE** *gets out her phone and starts looking.)*

MAEVE. So the kids know?

AIDAN. You really think the campers know and we wouldn't have heard anything about it?

BECCA. At least Kylie knows. Maybe she hasn't told anyone?

CASSIE. *(As she scrolls.)* I told you. She's mature. But she's not tweeting.

This guy replied to her at 4:05, and she wrote back to him twenty minutes later. We were braiding friendship tourniquets that whole time. I had eyes on her. This isn't her.

LUKAS. Could it be her management?

CASSIE. They don't have access to her socials. Authenticity is a huge part of her brand.

MAEVE. Do you think it's her parents?

BECCA. Well I hope it's not her parents, because Truth Squad people do not like what she's posting. And they say they're gonna find her. To re-educate her. And also keep her safe from pedophiles? And um...

MAEVE. What?

BECCA. Someone posted our website.

(Pause. This sets in.)

AIDAN. I don't see how they could know she's here. Right?

(Silence.)

MAEVE. Aidan, I think you should get Linda.

AIDAN. It's late. We don't need to –

MAEVE. We need to get Linda. Now.

*(**AIDAN** starts to walk away from the circle. He speaks into his walkie.)*

AIDAN. Linda...

(To himself.) I can't do this.

(He turns back to them.)

I can't do this. I'm sorry.

She's gone. She left.

BECCA. Well, we'll tell her when she gets back.

AIDAN. I don't think she's coming back.

It's been almost two weeks.

LUKAS. Where'd she go?

AIDAN. I think her family's in New Kansas.

MAEVE. Why didn't you tell us?

AIDAN. You were all stepping up. I was trying to, too.
And mostly I could figure things out.
But this...this...

(He falls into silence, shaking his head.)

LUKAS. I'm just trying to understand what's real right now. Like, those town hall meetings you said CDL was at. They're not real?

AIDAN. No, they're real. She just stopped going. There's a $50 fine now for "Disturbing the Night." I wouldn't worry about it though. Everyone's moving out. I've been taking the golf cart around the lake, trying to see if we can set up some sort of community emergency plan. So we can all keep each other safe if anything happens. But they've all bought new houses in Canada.

LUKAS. Dang.

AIDAN. I asked if we could use their basements if we needed to shelter, but they said no. They were worried about their insurance. And their carpeting.

BECCA. Cassie, what about your parents?

AIDAN. What about them?

MAEVE. They have a place on the lake.

AIDAN. Which house? Have I met them?

CASSIE. *(Insisting.)* They're definitely out of town.

BECCA. It's the forest green one with big windows? All the way on the southern bank?

AIDAN. I don't think that's right.

BECCA. She took me to see it.

AIDAN. I think that's the house I had to babysit those kids in.

CASSIE. Really?

BECCA. You're probably thinking of a different house. They have a boat.

AIDAN. The Second Chance?

(Pause.)

CASSIE. Maybe they were renting the place out?

AIDAN. There were pictures of the kids all over the walls.

(Pause.)

MAEVE. Cassie, do your parents live on the lake?

(Pause.)

CASSIE. *(Raw.)* Some things are private, okay? I understand you're stressed and a lot is going on but you're being really intense, and like, I just don't wanna talk about it. Does that make sense?

LUKAS. I think what doesn't make sense to me is if your parents don't live on the lake why you would even come here.

CASSIE. I... I, um...

BECCA. Yeah, wait, what?

MAEVE. Why are you lying to us?

CASSIE. I don't –

MAEVE. You told us you didn't believe in lying. And we believed you.

BECCA. What's going on?

CASSIE. I want to tell a scary story.

AIDAN. We don't have time to –

CASSIE. Once someone starts a scary story, you can't talk until it's over. You have to stop what you're doing and listen.

(Everyone is silent. They uncross their arms.)

There once was a little girl who had to live with her grandparents when her parents were out of town on business. And her grandpa was dying in a slow and awful way. Her grandma would try to comfort her, singing a song about how everybody's got to go sometime. And her grandma would take her to the Goodwill donation box and have her drop bags of her grandpa's things into it one by one, because, she said, he wouldn't need them where he was going. When her grandpa wouldn't eat, the little girl would kneel on his chest and try to feed him, but he'd just choke. And it was like that for weeks, until he died.

And her grandma got really sad, and unplugged the phone so people would stop calling to say they were sorry, and told the girl to pack her things and took her into the middle of the woods.

The little girl met other kids there, the first she'd seen in months. But after her first night, the looks and giggling and pointing started. And she'd wake up in the middle of the night in places she didn't recognize, and missed her grandpa so much, and felt so scared. And one night her counselor tied her to her bed while her bunkmates watched, and then somehow she woke up on the floor, with a little girl standing over her, dirt and spit dripping down her chin, screaming that she wouldn't sleep one more night in the same room as that thing.

So she was moved to a shed that they cleared the chairs out of, and forced to stay awake. But one night she snuck out and walked back to her cabin. She wanted to prove to them that she had never meant to hurt anyone, so that maybe they would let her be in the bunk again.

When she got there, Jocelyn was smoking a cigarette on the porch. Jocelyn saw her, and thought she was sleeping, and threw her cigarette on the ground and ran at her. And the little girl tried to run but tripped and fell, and the cigarette fell in a pile of leaves under the porch, and it wasn't long until the flames started spreading. And pinning her to the ground, Jocelyn looked in her eyes and said, "You did this," before getting up and running into the cabin to help the other girls.

The little girl's parents finally picked her up, and she swore she would never go back to that horrible place. But she was little then. One day, she'll decide it's time to make peace with who she is.

So she'll get a job. She'll show up for day one. She'll believe that she really has changed. And then she'll hear a story.

And she'll lose her sleeping medication.

And it'll start all over again.

And she'll try to stay awake to keep herself from doing the awful things she knows she's capable of. But she won't be able to.

She'll hear that they're planning to keep watch for someone in the woods and she'll make them decaf coffee with ground-up Benadryl.

She'll realize that she would still do anything to just be one of them.

And she'll realize that she hasn't really changed at all.

And that maybe nothing ever does.

All there is is living with it.

(Dead silence.)

MAEVE. Cassie.

*(**CASSIE** doesn't look up.)*

We didn't know.

CASSIE. I know.

MAEVE. I'm so sorry. I'm so sorry that happened to you. And for the part I played in it.

(Pause.)

And at the same time, I don't know how we can ever trust you again.

CASSIE. I didn't know how I could trust you again, and I'm still trying.

LUKAS. I... I don't... I don't... I don't know...what to do with that. It's so...big. The size of how much this place hurt you and... I guess...how much I love it here? And how much it's done for me? And if I acknowledge that, does that mean...does that mean I'm saying what it did to you was worth it? 'Cause I... I can't...

MAEVE. *(Not wanting to shirk responsibility.)* We can't hide behind, like... Like, "this place" didn't... Like, *people* did this, you know?

AIDAN. But they did it here. And maybe if they were somewhere else, they wouldn't have. I don't know. I don't... I can't believe you came back.

CASSIE. Everyone always told me it was probably just a tough situation where everyone was doing the best they could. And I wanted to do better than they did, 'cause then I'd know it wasn't true.

I didn't know you'd all be here. I didn't mean for this to be so...literal.

BECCA. *(Gently.)* I'm glad you came back. I'm glad I got to meet you.

I'm sorry I got you sent to the chair shed.

CASSIE. I'm sorry I almost killed you.

For what it's worth, in my head I was trying to save your life.

(Pause.)

CASSIE. Wow. Apologies feel so inadequate.

LUKAS. I know. I'm sorry. I mean, yeah.

MAEVE. But I guess I don't know what else to do.
I wanna step up.
I wanna go above and beyond.
But there are people coming to maybe kill us.
And I'm... What if nothing's enough?

(Silence.)

BECCA. Point of order. I request the floor.

(Pause.)

AIDAN. The floor is granted.

BECCA. I have a concern. We don't know how to make this better right now, and we may never get to, because there are people coming to maybe kill us. And all we have to defend ourselves, all we're good at are the things we've always done, and the ways we've always done them, and clearly that's not enough, and never was. So, my proposed solution, and I know there's problems with this, but my solution is: We initiate the Super-Secret Ultimate Overnight Hike-A-Thon. Tonight. Now.

LUKAS. The problem... I see...

Okay. There are still like a hundred campers here, and twenty counselors. That's a really big group. We're gonna be very noticeable as we move, and it's gonna be hard to move together.

So. So. My solution. We leave at staggered times. Oldest kids first, 'cause they can get ready fastest, and have the longest legs, and the most skills. Then we can mark a trail and clear the path and set up camps for the younger kids as we go. We'll all end up in the same place each night, but then everyone can do what's right for them.

MAEVE. My turn. Right. Ummm...

We're gonna be at the front of the trail, then. And I don't know how we're gonna know where to go. We can't have our phones. They could track us, if they want to follow us. And without our phones, we can't communicate or find out where they're coming from or where we should be heading to get the kids to safety.

My solution is: We have the long-distance radio transmitter in the office. If someone can operate that, we could get a signal on the crank radios. But if we wanna do that, someone would have to stay behind.

AIDAN. I can do it.

MAEVE. Aidan –

AIDAN. *(Simply.)* I don't have any campers.

Or maybe I have all the campers.

I might technically be the camp director now.

(Pause.)

All right, the problem I see is, the kids.

They're not gonna be able to do this.

LUKAS. You saw them today, they're –

AIDAN. Yeah, yeah they're amazing, but they're kids.

They're not responsible for anyone but themselves.

And as long as they think that way, something is gonna go wrong and people are gonna get hurt.

My solution is: We tell them.

It won't be camp anymore. It'll become something really different. And maybe we need it to be something really different.

Cassie?

(Silence.)

CASSIE. I don't see any problem with that.

BECCA. Do any other delegates have remaining concerns?

ALL BUT BECCA. Nay.

BECCA. Then I move to close the floor.

MAEVE. Seconded.

BECCA. Shall we close the floor?

ALL BUT BECCA. Yea.

BECCA. The motion passes, the concern is resolved, the floor is closed.

(It starts to rain.)

CASSIE. And we're really gonna do this? Right now? For real?

AIDAN. *(An answer to* **CASSIE.***)* Phones.

(They each take a last look at their phones and quickly check the last things they want to check. They power them down and put them in the bucket.)

CASSIE. Okay, we should get moving.

(Everyone starts to move, but **LUKAS** *hangs back by the fire. He takes out his half-burnt paper, deciding whether or not to put it in the fire.* **MAEVE** *notices.)*

MAEVE. What is it?

LUKAS. Oh, uh...

(She takes it from him and reads it.)

MAEVE. "We are the living prophecies of the future we'll create."

(The rain becomes a downpour. She looks at **LUKAS**. *She puts the prophecy into the fire.)*

CASSIE. Let's go.

*(***MAEVE** *hugs* **AIDAN**. *The* **COUNSELORS** *leave.)*

*(***AIDAN** *sits down. He looks at the fire for a bit. He takes out his earpiece. He looks at the audience for the first time, and the rain stops.)*

AIDAN. This scary story is called The Ending.

You go off into the woods because something's coming. And it's too late to do anything to stop it.

You tread quietly and cover your tracks and whisper like you're afraid you'll spook the animals.

You move quickly, because all you want is to survive. You get a radio transmission that they're coming from the west, so you cut north. When you spot the helicopters above the treeline, you huddle under the camouflage quilts you macramed. And then you hear them shouting, and the dogs barking, coming from all around you, and you all plunge into the river, and into darkness. It's time to do what you practiced. You hold your breath and form a big human chain to keep everyone weighed down under the water. And you start to count. You know everyone can make it to 100. And those 100 seconds are all you have. You hear muted voices above the water. You hear gunfire. And then you hear nothing.

And then you swim to the surface. Not because you know that it's safe, but because you can't stay down any longer. You all swim to the surface, and they're gone. You did it. You survived.

You camp where you are for the next few days, hoping they won't come to the same place twice. And they don't. Yet. But now all the small people there with you start to look at you and ask, "What do we do now?" And you realize you were prepared for the worst, but not what happens after.

So you keep living. You find a new place to stay, and you make new rules and games and sing songs and tell stories. You try to do everything better this time, because now you understand that no one's around to do it for you.

But it doesn't work. Or it works very little.

You end up repeating so many of the mistakes of where you came from.

And you even make some things worse.

And as you're back in the woods running away from everything you made,

you're sure it's going to kill you.

But it doesn't.

You survive again.

And again.

Every time you think the world is ending, it doesn't.

It only almost does.

And you have to come back, and figure out how to live with everything you made and everyone you made it with.

But this time, a little better.

And every time, no matter how bad it gets, you keep living.

The scary part is you keep living.

Sometimes it feels impossible.

You feel too old and too young and everything is changing too much and not enough.

But when it feels impossible you have a system.

It works best if you close your eyes. I'll close mine too, to keep it equal.

(The audience and **AIDAN** *close their eyes, if they're willing.)*

What's gonna happen now is I'm gonna ask you some questions, and all you have to do is answer them in a way that feels true to you. You don't have to say anything out loud. Okay? Okay.

What are you going to miss most about the way things are right now?

(He lets the audience think.)

Can you see what you'll miss in your mind?

(He lets the audience think.)

Now imagine yourself a year from now and everything's different. Do you think you could find those things again if you really needed to?

(He lets the audience think.)

What do you hope to get out of everything that comes next?

(He lets the audience think.)

Can you think of one little thing you can do tomorrow to get you one step closer to your hope?

(He lets the audience think.)

Now that you have that to look forward to, do you think you can make it one more day?

(He lets the audience think.)

You can open your eyes whenever you want.

(As the audience does, they see that the fire is low, and **AIDAN** *is standing, holding his chair folded up under his arm.)*

AIDAN. There are no wrong answers. Only your answers.

And nature.

(He walks away from the clearing. The fire goes out. Darkness.)

End of Play

CPSIA information can be obtained
at www.ICGtesting.com
Printed in the USA
LVHW050449060723
751511LV00003B/180

9 780573 710001